jE   READERS

Get That Pest!

Illust ... **rt Yee**

Green Light Readers
Harcourt, Inc.
San Diego   New York   London

Mom and Pop Nash had ten red hens. Every day they got ten eggs.

One morning, five eggs were missing!

"Someone has robbed our hens!" shouted Pop.
"We can't let him get another egg!" said Mom.

The Nashes hid in the shed.

C-C-Crick. "What's that?" asked Mom.

A wolf slipped
into the shed.

He popped four
eggs into his sack.

"It's a wolf!" shouted Mom.
"I'll get him!" shouted Pop.

"Too bad," said Pop.
"Get this net off me!" shouted Mom.

Now only ONE egg was left.

"We have to get that pest!" said Mom.
"Help me set this trap," said Pop.
When the trap was set, they hid.

C-C-Crick...Smash!

The trap got Mom and Pop.
The wolf got the last egg.

Then Mom and Pop Nash set a
BIG trap and hid.

C-C-Crick…Womp!

"Let me out," begged the wolf. "You can have all the eggs back."
"You didn't eat them?" asked Pop.

"No," said the wolf. "I PAINTED them."
"Oh my!" said Mom.
"Well, well," said Pop.

Now Mom and Pop Nash sell
painted eggs. Would you like one?

Requests for permission to make copies of any part of the work should be mailed to:
Permissions Department, Harcourt, Inc., 6277 Sea Harbor Drive,
Orlando, Florida 32887-6777.

First Green Light Readers edition 2000
Green Light Readers is a registered trademark of Harcourt, Inc.

Library of Congress Cataloging-in-Publication Data
Douglas, Erin.
Get that pest!/Erin Douglas; illustrated by Wong Herbert Yee.
—1st Green Light Readers ed.
p. cm.
"Green Light Readers."
Summary: When a farmer and his wife discover that something is stealing the
eggs laid by their ten red hens, they set up elaborate traps to catch the thief.
[1. Eggs—Fiction. 2. Farm life—Fiction. 3. Stealing—Fiction.]
I. Yee, Wong Herbert, ill. II. Title.
PZ7.D74643Ge 2000
[E]—dc21 99-6801
ISBN 0-15-202548-0
ISBN 0-15-202554-5 (pb)

A C E G H F D B

A C E G H F D B (pb)

Meet the Illustrator

Wong Herbert Yee always wanted to be an artist. He started writing and illustrating children's books when he was an adult. His daughter is his helper. She tells him if she thinks other children will enjoy his stories.

Wong Herbert Yee